A WEEKEND AT THE GRAND HOTEL

MARY LABATT

KIDS CAN PRESS

Kids Can Press acknowledges the financial support of the Ontario Arts Council, the Canada Council for the Arts and the Government of Canada, through the BPIDP, for our publishing activity.

Published in Canada by
Kids Can Press Ltd.
29 Birch Avenue
Toronto, ON M4V 1E2

Published in the U.S. by
Kids Can Press Ltd.
2250 Military Rd.
Tonawanda, NY 14150

Edited by Charis Wahl
Designed by Marie Bartholomew
Typeset by Karen Birkemoe
Printed and bound in Canada

CM 01 0 9 8 7 6 5 4 3 2 1
CM PA 01 0 9 8 7 6 5 4 3 2 1

Canadian Cataloguing in Publication Data

Labatt, Mary, date.
   A weekend at the Grand Hotel

(Sam, dog detective)
ISBN 1-55074-883-1 (bound) ISBN 1-55074-885-8 (pbk.)

I. Title. II. Series: Labatt, Mary, date . Sam, dog detective.

PS8573.A135W43 2001   jC813'.54   C00.931637-X
PZ7.L32 We 2001

Kids Can Press is a Nelvana company

To my parents —
with my love

1. The Dog Food War

IT'S MADE OUT
OF CAT GUTS!

Sam woke up on Monday morning in a terrible mood. It had been a bad weekend. For two days Joan and Bob had tried to feed Sam dog food.

Sam sighed. *They should know better.*

To make things worse, Jennie's family had gone away for the weekend. Ten-year-old Jennie Levinsky was Sam's next-door neighbor and her best friend. Joan and Bob had hired Jennie to dog-sit Sam when they were at work. Jennie would have given Sam some real food.

Sam hopped off the spare bed. In the kitchen she glowered at Joan and Bob as they packed their lunches and rushed to work.

"I'll leave you some Liver Delight, Sam."

Joan put a dog bowl on the floor, grabbed her briefcase and dashed out the door.

Don't do me any favors, thought Sam savagely.

The door shut and Sam was alone. She eyed the dog food with disgust. *Let it rot.*

As the hours ticked by, Sam hopped off the sofa every once in a while and paced the house. *I'm bored. I'm a fabulous detective with no case. And I'm so hungry, I'm half dead.* Sam sighed loudly. *My life has hit bottom.*

At last the key turned in the lock and Jennie leaned around the living room doorway. She dropped her schoolbag in the hall. "Hi, Sam! I missed you! Beth's coming in a few minutes."

Sam looked dolefully at her friend. *You'll have to take me to the hospital soon. I'm starving. I'm going to faint.*

Jennie giggled.

Sam's thoughts rang in Jennie's head in a

hollow, echoing way. It was just like talking. No one else could hear Sam. Not even Jennie's best friend, Beth Morrison. Sam had told Jennie she had a special gift. *I can always tell when someone's got it. Most dogs are too stupid to notice.*

Jennie gave Sam a huge hug, but Sam just sniffed. *Go and look at the glop in my bowl.*

Jennie peered into the kitchen and wrinkled her nose. The Liver Delight was hard and crusty. "Ugh. That doesn't smell very good."

Not good? They make that stuff out of cat guts. And gopher guts and bits of run-over skunks off the road. Nobody should eat it!

Just then the doorbell rang. Beth ran into the living room and threw her arms around Sam's big neck. Sam slurped at Beth's fluffy red hair.

After a few licks, Sam stared at Jennie again. *Take me to your house, Jennie. I need food.*

When the three friends got to Jennie's house,

her thirteen-year-old brother, Noel, opened the door. "How's Samantha the walking mop?" He grinned at Sam.

Shut up, Oaf. Sam tried to push past Noel. *Lummox. Pimply faced teenager. Tell him to get out of my way, Jennie. I need some serious snacks.*

Noel grabbed his baseball and headed out the door. "Mom and Dad are working at the drugstore till five thirty, Jennie. Call me if you need me."

Sam marched straight to the kitchen and scratched at the cupboards. *How about cheese puffs with ketchup? I need sardines with ice cream. Hurry! I'm going to pass out.*

Jennie rooted through the fridge.

"Yuck!" cried Beth when Jennie poured ketchup over mint ice cream.

Jennie giggled as she filled bowls with leftovers. "Sam says she's starving. She had a rough weekend trying not to eat dog food."

Rough is not the word. It was hideous.

Sam slurped and chomped with loud happy smacks. *Whew! This is better.*

Upstairs in Jennie's room, Sam climbed up on the bed and belched. She lay back on Jennie's pillows.

She was just starting to doze when she thought of something that made her perk up. *Hey! I almost forgot. You're dog-sitting me this weekend.*

Jennie nodded. "Yup. You're staying at my house while Joan and Bob are away."

The hair over Sam's eyes lifted. *I hope you're planning to buy me loads of treats.*

"Don't worry, Sam." Jennie winked at Beth. "I promise I'll feed you good stuff."

Don't even mention dog food. I want fudge brownies and jelly doughnuts every day.

I haven't had a jelly doughnut in years.

2. The Levinskys Win a Prize

When Jennie's parents came home from their drugstore, they burst in the front door shouting, "Surprise!"

Jennie, Beth and Sam ran to the top of the stairs. Noel poked his head in from outside. "What is it?" they all asked.

"It's wonderful!" sang Mr. Levinsky, twirling his wife around in a little dance.

"Better than wonderful!" echoed Jennie's mom. "We've been selling Silky Soft hand lotion for years and we finally won one of their prizes."

"Prizes?" repeated Jennie blankly.

"We won a family weekend at the Grand Hotel!" shouted Jennie's dad. "It's the most expensive hotel in the country!"

"And," added Mrs. Levinsky, "we've got a royal suite!"

Mr. Levinsky whipped a brochure out of his pocket and waved it at them. "The prize is for a family of six! Jennie, that means you can take Beth, and Noel can take Jason!"

Jennie and Beth squealed with delight.

Hey! What about me?

But nobody was listening. "We've called the hotel and we're going this weekend!" Jennie's mother twirled around again.

Sam gasped and nudged Jennie's leg. *Wait a minute! You're dog-sitting me this weekend!*

"Uh-oh." Jennie's smile faded. "We promised to dog-sit Sam this weekend."

Mrs. Levinsky stopped twirling. "I forgot," she said, her hand to her mouth.

Sam bumped Jennie again. *Take me! I deserve to go to this fancy place just as much as Beth.*

When Jennie didn't answer, Sam glared at her. *I'm your friend, too.*

Jennie winced. "C-can I take Sam?"

Sam glared at the whole family. *I need a holiday once in a while. If anyone cares.*

"Take Sam?" Jennie's parents looked blank. "To a hotel?"

"Hotels don't take dogs," scoffed Noel. "Especially stupid-looking ones."

Sam glowered at him.

"Well …" Mr. Levinsky was scanning the brochure. "It says here the Grand is one of the few hotels that still allows dogs."

Jennie's mother peered over his shoulder. "You have to keep your dog on a leash."

Leash! I will not be dragged around on a leash!

"We'll worry about the leash later," Jennie whispered in Sam's ear.

Hmph.

"I guess we could take Sam." Jennie's father rubbed his chin thoughtfully. "I can't see what harm it would do."

No harm. I never do any harm.

"We'd have to ask Joan and Bob." Jennie's parents looked questioningly at each other.

Noel slumped against the wall. "I don't want

to go anywhere with this ridiculous dog."

Quiet, Lummox.

But Jennie's parents were thinking. "We could fit everybody in our new van," said Jennie's mother slowly.

"Then it's settled!" cried Jennie's father. "We're supposed to dog-sit Sam, so Sam goes with us — if Joan and Bob agree."

"Hurray!" shouted Jennie. "Did you hear that, Sam? You can come!"

Sam sniffed. *It's no more than I deserve.*

"Come on, Sam. Let's go ask Joan and Bob. They'll be home now."

Noel groaned. "I refuse to be seen with a kid who talks to dogs."

3. The Grand Hotel

I LOVE BEING RICH!

When the weekend arrived, they all scrambled into the Levinskys' new van.

"Everybody buckled up?" Jennie's dad backed out of the driveway. "Grand Hotel, here we come!"

Noel and his friend Jason sat in the middle seat with their earphones on. Jennie, Beth and Sam had the back seat to themselves.

Sam looked through the rear window. She loved the way the road rolled out behind them. As she watched, she hummed to herself.

When Jennie opened her window, Sam poked her nose outside. The wind whipped her fur into little points. Houses whistled past.

Trucks whooshed by. *Now, this is life!*

The buildings got taller and taller. At last Mr. Levinsky veered off on a smooth highway that curved high in the air. Sam watched the teeming city glide by the windows.

I'll find a terrific mystery here. Sam shivered happily. *Cities are full of mysteries.*

After a while the van pulled to a stop in front of an elegant stone building.

Uniformed doormen held the doors of limousines, and beautifully dressed people stepped out. Some wore sunglasses. Others were swathed in jewelry. While porters scurried behind them with luggage, they sailed through the gilt and glass doors.

This is good.

"How do you do, sir and madam?" asked a doorman holding the van door wide. Mrs. Levinsky smiled and stepped out.

The side door was opened. Noel and Jason climbed out, their earphones hanging from their ears, a startled look on their faces.

"And how are the young sirs today?" smiled

the doorman.

The young sirs are idiots. Never mind them. We want out.

"Aha!" beamed the doorman. "Two young ladies and a dog."

You bet. I'm here all right.

The doorman produced a leash from his pocket and snapped it on Sam's collar.

Watch it. I might bite.

"Put up with it," whispered Jennie. "We'll take it off later."

Phooey. I should show this guy my wonderful teeth.

When they got to the hotel lobby, Sam felt as if she had stepped into a fairy tale. Her eyes swept over brocade sofas, crystal chandeliers, deep crimson rugs, marble floors and enormous china lamps. Here and there in silken armchairs, people were reading newspapers or chatting while they sipped tea from dainty cups.

Sam stuck her nose high in the air. *This is where a beautiful dog like me belongs.*

The family stood in a little group while Mr. Levinsky went to register.

Then two porters whisked them into walnut and brass elevators, and they whooshed to the tenth floor. When the elevator doors silently slid open, Sam peered out. More crystal chandeliers, crimson carpets and pale blue brocade walls. The hallway was as elegant as the lobby.

A porter stopped at a carved oak door and stuck a door card into the slot. "Here you are, Mr. and Mrs. Levinsky."

When Sam and the girls followed Jennie's parents into the suite, their jaws dropped. It was beautiful. Polished tables with huge vases of flowers, gilt mirrors and deep satiny armchairs.

I love being rich.

Jennie and Beth scurried around opening doors. Gleaming bathrooms and luxurious bedrooms appeared.

Quick! Grab a bedroom that looks at the city! Sam shoved in front and dashed for a window with a view. She put her paws on the windowsill and looked down at the rolling traffic. Far below, people scurried to and fro.

Sam hopped up on the bed and settled her head on a satin pillow.

This is great, Jennie. Open your suitcase and bring out the snacks.

4. Sam Discovers Room Service

I CAN'T WAIT TO ORDER SOMETHING.

As Sam chomped on spicy nacho chips, she heard Mr. Levinsky dial the phone in the living room. He said something about pizza. Sam's ears pricked up.

"That's right," said Mr. Levinsky. "We're the family that won the Silky Soft prize weekend. I understand we have unlimited room service."

"What's room service?" asked Jennie.

It's got something to do with pizza.

"You phone down to order food," said Beth. "We went to a hotel once, and they brought breakfast on a table with wheels."

Sam sat up. *Phoning for food is good. Listen.*

"Perfect," Mr. Levinsky was saying. "Six sundaes and three large pizzas."

No sundae for me? Sam whirled on Jennie. *See how humans treat me!*

"Never mind," soothed Jennie. "You can have some of mine."

Phooey. I want a huge one all to myself!

Half an hour later, Sam, Jennie and Beth crowded in the bedroom doorway as the waiter wheeled in a narrow table. The table was set with flowers and elegant china. The gleaming white tablecloth hung to the floor.

Sam watched the table glide over the thick carpet. *I can hide under that tablecloth. You can pass food to me.*

As the family helped themselves to pizza, Sam slipped under the tablecloth. *Perfect. I'll eat all my meals under here.*

So, Jennie ... Hurry up with the pizza.

While they ate, the family talked excitedly about what they wanted to do in the city. Jason and Noel wanted to visit all the music superstores.

Good. We're rid of them.

Jennie's mother and father wanted to shop.

Tell them we don't want to shop.

"We don't want to shop," repeated Jennie obediently.

"We could all go to the theater later," suggested Jennie's mother.

They don't let dogs in theaters.

"We don't want to do that either," said Jennie.

Beth's green eyes widened with surprise. "We don't?"

"No, we don't," said Jennie firmly.

"Oh." Beth thought for moment. "What do we want to do, then?"

We want to explore the hotel. We don't want to go anywhere.

"Can we look around the hotel?" Jennie asked.

Beth grinned. "That's what Sam wants, isn't it?" she whispered.

Jennie giggled.

Mr. Levinsky's eyebrows shot up. "Are you sure that's what you want to do?"

Jennie and Beth both smiled happily. "We're sure."

"It doesn't sound like much fun to me." Jennie's mother was doubtful. She looked at her husband.

He shrugged. "Well ... maybe the hotel has some kind of baby-sitting service. Someone to check on the kids."

We don't want anybody checking on us.

"We don't need a baby-sitter, Dad," said Jennie seriously. "We won't even go outside."

After some discussion, Jennie's parents agreed to let the girls stay at the hotel while they went shopping. "Don't get into trouble though," Mrs. Levinsky warned. "This hotel is a big place."

Quit worrying. When did we ever get into trouble?

"Be careful," added Jennie's father.

Phooey. We're always careful.

Jennie and Beth winked at each other.

Under the table, Sam chortled happily to herself as she gobbled the last bit of pizza.

When everyone was gone, Jennie and Beth got ready to explore the hotel. Sam licked all the plates and sundae dishes.

"I'm a little scared," said Jennie as she shoved the door card in her pocket. "I don't want to get lost."

Beth was confident. "We won't. We're on the tenth floor. Room 1014. How can we get lost?"

Jennie hesitated, chewing her lip nervously.

Sam sniffed the edge of the door. She turned around crossly and stepped impatiently from foot to foot. *Quit stalling, Jennie. This is a city. There's adventure out there.*

Beth snapped on Sam's leash.

Sam glared. *Tell this kid not to drag me around, Jennie.*

One yank and I bite.

5. Sam Finds a Mystery

The empty hallway seemed to stretch forever. Silently Jennie, Beth and Sam padded along the thick red carpet and pushed the bell for the elevator.

With a ding, the elevator doors slid back, and the three friends got in. Their stomachs flipped as they were whisked down ten floors. When the doors opened, they stepped out onto the gleaming marble floor of the lobby. Sitting in the silk chairs or clustered around gilt pillars were people who looked as if they had come from all over the world.

Fascinated, Jennie, Beth and Sam wandered through the lobby.

Let's sit here. Sam stopped in front of a huge silk sofa and started to climb up.

Jennie reached over and pulled on the leash. "You have to sit on the floor, Sam!"

The hair over Sam's eyes lifted in surprise. *You've got to be kidding.*

Jennie shook her head. "I'm not kidding! If you sit on the couch, they'll kick us out."

Sam looked around. *Rich people are so selfish. All I want to do is sit like a normal person.*

"You're not a person. You're a dog."

Beth giggled. "No, she's not! Just ask her."

Sam glared. *I'll tell you what I am. I'm a famous detective.* She looked around hopefully. *This is a good place for a detective. Crooks hang around fancy places like this.*

Jennie and Beth perched on the edge of the sofa while Sam lolled on the small carpet at their feet.

When a beautiful blond woman walked past, Jennie nudged Beth. "I bet she's a model."

Then Beth caught sight of a tall man carrying a guitar case. "He looks like a rock star!"

Jennie's brown eyes sparkled. "I want to see a famous movie actor."

Sam snorted. *Forget famous people. What we want is a mystery.*

A man in a cowboy hat clicked past, his boots ringing on the marble floor. A man in a turban looked at them. An airline pilot in a navy uniform strolled by. A lady in a long black dress and veil smiled at Sam with her eyes.

I love this. I was born to be rich.

Jennie searched the crowd. "There's got to be a movie star here."

Sam looked around happily. *There's got to be a great mystery in a place like this.*

Out of the corner of her eye, Sam glimpsed a man getting on the elevator with a big briefcase. *Hmm ... I bet that's filled with tools to break open a safe.*

Then she noticed a gentleman in a gray suit tweak his white mustache and cross his elegant legs. A folded newspaper lay across his lap. *Who's that guy waiting for? I bet he's a spy.*

Behind the man, a woman in a mink coat was

walking a white poodle.

Sam stared intently at the poodle. *Hey, dog! Have you tried room service yet?*

The dog didn't turn in Sam's direction.

Can't hear me. Sam sniffed. *I always knew poodles were stupid.*

Sam watched the poodle's owner carefully. *That lady is looking at everybody's jewelry! She's a jewel thief if I ever saw one.*

Suddenly porters moved from all sides of the lobby toward the front doors. Sam turned to watch. *Oh-ho! Somebody important is coming.*

The manager rushed out of his office and motioned to the porters.

Sam sat up straight and craned her neck. *Maybe it's a king.*

"Could be a millionaire," breathed Jennie.

"Or a movie star," added Beth.

I love this place. Why waste time shopping when you can see all this?

Through the doors came a well-dressed man and woman. She was wearing a light blue dress. He wore a dark business suit and carried a briefcase. They nodded importantly to the manager. Behind them lagged a boy of about ten. He looked very, very bored.

These people don't look special.

Jennie shrugged. "Maybe they're big deals in the government or something."

Government ... Hmm ... Which government? Maybe he's a spy ... Maybe he's meeting that spy over there with the mustache.

Sure enough, the man with the mustache nodded at the newcomers.

Looks like a signal. Sam sniffed at the new arrivals as they walked past. *Mighty suspicious ...*

Just then, one of the porters reached for the man's briefcase. But he refused to let the porter take it.

Did you see that? Sam stood up to get a better look. *I bet the briefcase is full of secret stuff!*

Smiling, the manager led the family to the elevator. Jennie and Beth smiled shyly at the boy, but he wouldn't look at them.

Forget the kid. I think we've landed in a nest of spies.

Sam was thinking about spies when someone else caught her eye. In a corner of the lobby, peering out from behind a gilt column, was a sneaky-looking man in a dark suit. He had something on his ear, with a wire going down into his collar.

Look at that! Another spy! Hmm ... That's weird. This one's got a hearing aid.

Jennie's eyes followed Sam's. The sneaky man muttered into his shirtfront.

He talks to himself. That's even weirder.

The man narrowed his eyes and stared hard at the important family.

Hey! He's not friendly to them! He must be a spy for the other side!

Sam's heart soared and her head buzzed with excitement. *Here's my new mystery, Jennie! This hotel is full of spies and I'm going to catch them!*

Sam could see her picture on the front page of the newspaper. The headline screamed, WONDER DOG CATCHES DANGEROUS SPY RING. Sam hummed to herself and stepped back and forth in a happy little dance.

I'll get a medal ... I've always wanted a medal.

Jennie groaned. "Beth, you won't believe what Sam's talking about."

"Oh yes I would!" laughed Beth, watching the sneaky man mutter into his collar. "Sam's found a new mystery. Haven't you, Sam?"

Sam slurped at Beth's small chin. *You bet. And it's a good one!*

6. Spies Everywhere

THEY'RE SELLING SECRETS!

Quick! Let's follow the new people!

Sam trotted toward an elevator, with Jennie and Beth close behind. When they got there, Jennie looked quizzically at Sam.

Tenth floor. Same as us.

"How do you know?"

I heard the porter say so. I've got great ears. Remember?

Jennie pressed "10" and the elevator whooshed upward.

They stepped out on the same floor they had left an hour earlier. The new family was walking slowly down the hallway.

Against one wall stood a housekeeping cart

stacked with towels and cleaning supplies. *Hide here! We'll watch where they go.*

Just as the three friends squeezed in behind the cart, the elevator dinged and the doors opened. Two porters pushing a luggage cart rushed to catch up with the family. Far down the hall, they turned a corner and disappeared from sight.

Sam leaped out from behind the cart. *We need to know what suite they're in.* She dashed after the porters, her leash trailing along the carpet.

At the corner Sam stopped and peered around. Down the hall, the porters were opening a door for the newcomers.

Then the door clicked shut and the hallway was empty.

Sam ran to the door and stared back at the girls. *Get the number, Jennie. You know I hate reading.*

Quickly the girls caught up. "It's 1062," Jennie read.

Good. Now we know where to find them.

The doorknob rattled.

"Sam! Let's go!" Jennie hissed. "I don't want

them to see us."

The door opened a crack and a voice came out of the room, "Thank you very much, sir. I hope your stay at the Grand Hotel is a pleasant one."

The door opened a bit farther.

Run! Sam dashed back, wheeled around the corner and wedged in behind the cleaning cart again. Jennie and Beth squeezed in after her.

Voices came closer and closer. Then the empty luggage cart appeared.

"Strange guy, huh?" one of the porters said as he walked past.

Sam's ears pricked up.

"Yeah," agreed the other porter. "You'd think that briefcase was full of gold."

"Did you see the way he snatched it?"

"Very weird."

Hmm … Sounds like he grabbed the briefcase again. Suspicious … Sam's mind whirred. *That settles it. He's definitely a spy. And that briefcase is filled with secrets!*

Sam thought about all the spy movies she'd

watched on TV. *I need a little camera to take pictures of the papers in his briefcase.*

She looked up to see Jennie glaring at her. "No way, Sam! We're not getting into trouble. We promised."

Sam sniffed.

Who said anything about trouble?

7. Spying on Spies

THIS IS SERIOUS.

"I knew Sam could find a mystery!" exclaimed Beth as she bounced on the silk bedspread.

Jennie rolled her eyes. "She thinks she found spies."

I did find spies. Loads of them.

"Maybe she did!" Beth grinned. "That guy with the ear piece was sure weird."

Exactly.

Beth stopped bouncing and hugged her knees thoughtfully. "I wonder why that man wouldn't let anybody touch his briefcase."

Because he's a spy. It's full of stolen secrets.

Jennie wasn't impressed. "Don't think about spies, Sam. Spies are dangerous."

Phooey. Forget dangerous. Sam looked around

for some food. *A new mystery makes me hungry. Call up room service. I want apple pie smothered in shrimps. And I want bologna with grape jelly.*

"I can't call room service, Sam."

Why not? It goes with the prize.

Jennie squirmed. "Um … I think it's just for grown-ups."

Sam fixed Jennie with a hard stare. *Room service, Jennie. Tell them I want ketchup on the side.*

Jennie sighed. "I hate the way you boss me around."

And I hate the way you let me starve.

When the waiter came with the trolley, he gave Jennie a strange look. He lifted the food covers and peered inside. "Apple pie with shrimps on top?"

Jennie nodded firmly. "I love it."

The waiter raised one bushy black eyebrow. "And bologna with grape jelly?"

Jennie reddened.

"That's mine!" sang Beth cheerfully. "I eat it once a week!"

The waiter raised his other eyebrow. "Okay, I believe you." Without another word, he turned and left the room. "Crazy kids," he muttered as the door closed behind him.

Jennie put the food on the floor for Sam.

Yum. Sam settled down to crunch and chomp. *Ptooey!* She spat out something hard. A shrimp tail landed on the carpet.

"Hey!" cried Jennie. "Don't make a mess. We'll get in trouble."

Sam looked puzzled. *Who's making a mess?*

Another shrimp tail sailed through the air. This time it landed on the sofa. Jennie scurried after it.

When Sam was finished, she belched and went over to the door. *Open it. I have to check out these spies.*

"Forget spies," said Jennie, fiddling with the remote control. "Let's watch TV."

Boring. Sam scratched at the door and

whined. *I found a great mystery and I'm going to solve it. I'll watch TV when I retire.*

Beth opened the door. "I think Sam wants to go out." She winked at Sam. "Let's go, Sam."

With a sigh, Jennie followed her friends.

Sam headed down the hall toward suite 1062. She turned the corner and hid behind the cleaning cart. Jennie and Beth followed.

"This is a big waste of time," muttered Jennie. "I don't want to spend my holiday stuck behind a bunch of towels."

"Shh!" said Beth. "I think I hear something."

An exit door at the end of the hall opened and the elegant man with the white mustache appeared. In his hand he carried a large brown envelope. Very quietly the man moved down the hall, looking at each room number. In front of suite 1062, he stopped and knocked.

The three friends held their breath.

The boy opened the door. "Yes?" he said politely, looking up at the stranger.

"Hello, Alexander. I have something for your father," said the man in a soft voice.

"I'll give it to him." Alexander held out his hand.

The man gave the boy the envelope, thanked him and turned back down the hall.

Behind the cleaning cart, Sam chortled. *Just like I thought.*

Jennie frowned. "It does look like they're passing secrets, doesn't it?"

"I wonder what kind of secrets spies steal." Beth chewed a fingernail as she watched the man disappear through the exit door.

I watched a show about it on TV. Spies steal stuff about governments and armies.

"Yeah." Jennie thought of movies she'd seen. "Sam's right. Spies steal the computer plans for weapons."

Beth nodded. "I get it. Stuff to win wars."

Yeah …

Like bombs.

8. A Conference for Spies

WHAT DID I TELL YOU?

When the three friends went back downstairs, the lobby was still crowded with interesting people.

The lady in black smiled at Sam again. A collie pranced past. A man in a jogging suit got on the elevator, just as the man wearing a turban got off.

After a few minutes, another elevator dinged. The man who got off was the one who had given Alexander the envelope.

Hmm ... There he is again. I'm calling that guy Mustache.

Sam watched Mustache stroll through the lobby. When he passed a pillar, the sneaky man with the ear-wire nodded at him.

Hey! He and Sneaky know each other!

The elevator dinged again and another man in a dark suit with an ear-wire got off.

Another one! I'll call this new guy Ear-Wire.

Ear-Wire walked to the other side of the lobby and looked around. Then he nodded to Sneaky. Sneaky nodded back.

Wow! Look at those signals!

Mustache returned with a newspaper and stood for a moment, stroking his beautiful white mustache.

Sam scowled. *I bet Mustache is hiding another envelope under that newspaper. Let's see what he does.*

Mustache walked over to the elevator and stepped on.

We have to follow him!

Sam raced across the lobby and reached the elevator just as the door closed. *Drat. Get the next one.*

Another elevator opened with a ding.

Quick! Press ten, Jennie. I think he's taking something to Alexander's father.

Up they went. But when the elevator doors opened, everything was different. Instead of pale blue walls, the hallway was dark green. Instead of crimson, the rug was gold. Instead of crystal, the chandeliers were brass.

Sam poked her head out. *Hey! Where are we?*

"I think we're on the wrong floor," muttered Beth.

Jennie squinted up at the numbers. "We're on eleven. I must have pressed the wrong button."

"Look!" Beth leaned out the door. "Something's going on at the end of the hall!" She pointed to a crowd of people milling around.

Sam shoved past her. *I want to see.*

"Sam!" called Jennie, but Sam dashed down the hall. Jennie sighed. "We have to follow her, Beth."

When the three friends got near the people, they ducked into an alcove where there was a pop machine and an ice dispenser. Many of the men and women were dressed in business suits.

Some wore jeans. Others wore long robes.

Jennie, Beth and Sam listened to the low murmuring voices. Every once in a while they caught a snippet of conversation.

"... great conference."

Hey! This is some kind of conference.

"... never thought I'd learn so much in three days."

"... can't wait to take this information home."

"... latest in nuclear techniques."

Nuclear! Sam pricked up her ears and strained to hear more.

A man strolled by with a folder under his arm. Sam peered at the printing on the cover. *What does it say, Jennie?*

For a minute, Jennie didn't answer.

Sam nudged her hand. *Tell me. You know I hate reading.*

Jennie tilted her head to read the title. "Nuclear something. I can't see it all."

Nuclear! Sam stared up at Jennie in shock. *That guy over there is talking about nuclear stuff, too! Nuclear means bombs!*

"Bombs?"

Beth's eyes widened. "Is Sam talking about nuclear bombs?"

Jennie nodded.

That's it! This is some kind of nuclear conference and spies are stealing nuclear secrets!

"What's a nuclear secret?" Jennie asked.

How you make bombs, of course.

"Nuclear bombs are terrible." Beth looked worried.

Sam turned toward Jennie, the hair over her eyes lifting up and down.

Let me tell you something, Jennie ...

Nobody needs nuclear secrets unless they're planning to blow up the world.

9. Sam Sets out Alone

I'M NOT HANGING AROUND HERE.

Back in the suite, Sam insisted on a snack. *This is a serious mystery and I need serious food.*

Jennie and Beth flipped on the TV and tried not to think about nuclear bombs. Jennie didn't want to call room service, but Sam insisted. At last Jennie gave in.

This time the waiter looked even more horrified. Sam glared at him while he checked the food.

When Sam had polished off the last butter tart topped with sardines, she turned to stare at her friends.

We're not hanging around here, are we?

No answer. Four teenage boys were singing

on television.

Come on! We can't sit around all day.

Jennie and Beth didn't move.

This is life and death, guys! People get blown up by these nuclear things. Whole cities get flattened.

But Beth and Jennie were smiling stupidly at the TV.

What's the matter with you two?

Sam nudged them both with her round black nose.

Excuse me. There are nuclear spies out there. I'd like to do something about it. I'd like my picture on the front page of the newspaper. I'd like a medal. And a big prize from the United Nations ... I'd like to be the most famous dog detective in the world ... Hello-o.

But Jennie and Beth just looked over Sam's head at the TV.

"I think Jo-Jo's the cutest," Jennie gushed.

Beth's green eyes were dreamy. "I love Jon-Jon. He's so sweet."

In disgust Sam looked at the screen. *None of those geeks are sweet. I'm sweet. And smart. And beautiful. Those turkeys are teenagers!*

But Jennie didn't answer.

Sam paced wildly. *I'm about to solve a huge mystery. It's going to change the history of the world!* She looked sideways at the girls. They were in a trance.

This is ridiculous.

Just then there was a knock on the door. Then another. The door opened and the maid called. When no one answered, she came in with a cleaning cart. After she wheeled it into a bedroom, Sam noticed something about the door. It didn't look right.

She sniffed at the edges. The door wasn't quite closed!

She pulled at it with her paw. Silently the door swung open. Sam looked back at Jennie and Beth. They were still staring at the television.

You watch those goofs. Sam stepped into the hall. *I'm out of here.*

See you later.

10. Following Alexander

SOMETHING'S VERY WEIRD.

Sam trotted down the long empty hallway. When she got to the corner, she stopped and peered around.

Alexander was coming out of suite 1062. And he had a large envelope under one arm.

Aha!

Alexander turned toward the door at the end of the hall.

Hmm.

Sam darted out and squeezed through the door just before it closed.

She found herself in a dimly lit stairwell. Ahead of her, Alexander was heading down the cement stairs. His footsteps rang in the empty space.

He must be doing something sneaky.

Keeping close to the brick walls, Sam followed. The stairs turned at each floor. Down, down, down, Sam tiptoed.

Alexander finally stopped at a big steel door, pushed the bar and the door opened. Sam slipped out behind him.

Outside, Sam reeled. Bright sunlight, cars, buses, strollers, honking, old people, young people, kids on Rollerblades, bicycles. The street was teeming with noise.

Weaving in and out through the crowd, Sam followed Alexander. At last he stopped in front of a store. Sam slunk behind a newspaper box and watched him go in.

Through the plate-glass window, Sam could see photocopiers and computers. Hmm ... Alexander passed the envelope to a man behind the counter.

Brilliant. That guy looks so ordinary nobody would ever be suspicious. I know who he is. He's the head spy.

Sam watched the head spy pull papers out of Alexander's envelope and feed them into a photocopier. She could see copies popping out into a tray.

He's photocopying secrets! He passes them to other spies ... just like on TV.

The man sorted papers, stapled them and put them in a new envelope.

I know what this is. It's a center for spies.

Alexander came out of the store and headed back toward the hotel. But Sam didn't follow.

I'll go around to the back and look for clues.

Dodging between shoppers, joggers and strollers, Sam trotted down the street in the other direction. She turned the corner and saw an alley. Garbage cans, boxes and parked trucks were everywhere. Delicious smells filled her nostrils. *Spaghetti. Roast beef. Sweet and sour chicken. Cities are wonderful. Cities are filled with food and robbers and criminals and spies ... I love cities.*

Sam sniffed up and down the alleyway, but she couldn't find the back of the spy's store. Each new smell was better than the last. *Hot dogs ... barbecued pork ... pizza ... tacos ... more pizza.* She was starving.

Sam's sniffing brought her out to a street. *So, where's the spy center?* She walked in one direction. Then she turned and walked the other way. Nothing looked familiar.

Sam stopped. *Uh-oh.*

Where's the hotel?

11. Lost in the City

PHOOEY.
I WAS NEVER
WORRIED.

Sam trotted back and forth trying to find a familiar scent, but she couldn't get past the food smells. At a corner, she stepped off the curb and followed a stream of people across the street. *Maybe it's this way.*

When she got to the other side, the gates of a huge park loomed in front of her. *Uh-oh. Wrong way.*

Sam turned and pushed her way back through the crowd. People bumped into her. Traffic whizzed by.

A car swooshed past her nose and Sam leaped back onto the curb. *Whew!*

She looked in every direction, but nothing

seemed familiar. Her head started to spin. The tall buildings seemed to sway dizzily around her.

Panic gripped her. Her nose filled with hundreds of different smells. Whirling around, Sam started down the street in the other direction, tripped over a ladder and sprawled on the pavement.

"That dog's going to step in the paint!" shouted a painter.

"Grab it!" called a lady pushing a stroller. "That dog looks lost!"

Sam scrambled to her feet. *Nobody's grabbing me, lady.*

Leaping between two parked cars, Sam darted into the traffic. Brakes screeched. Horns honked. Screams and shouts echoed from all sides.

"Watch where you're going!" A man shook his cane at Sam.

"Hey, dog!" shouted a taxi driver. "You want to get killed?"

Frantically Sam dashed for the sidewalk. Through the crowds she ran, crashing into a sign for a flower cart.

"Dumb mutt!" grumbled the flower seller as he picked up his sign.

Sam's head spun. People, cars and buildings melted together crazily. Quickly, she ducked under a parked truck to hide.

Crouching behind one of the wheels, Sam listened to her heart pounding wildly in her ears.

As hundreds of feet tromped by, Sam stuck her nose out and sniffed. *Gas, oil, roast beef, leather, dust, old newspapers, barbecued chicken, candy wrappers, rubber tires, perfume, sweat, hot dogs, popcorn, cola cans* ... A million smells wafted into Sam's nostrils.

Terror rose in her. *I won't be able to find my way back! There's too many smells!*

Sam's thoughts tumbled through her head. *I'm doomed.*

Tears sprang to Sam's eyes. *Jennie and Beth are never around when I need them.* Sam began to think terrible thoughts about her friends. *They're probably having room service and watching those teenage oafs on TV. What do they care that I'm lost in a dangerous city? What ——*

Just then, Sam caught a familiar whiff. She breathed deeply. *I've smelled that shoe polish before.*

A pair of shiny brown oxfords walked toward her. Sam sniffed again.

Hmm … Two smells together … Leather and lemon aftershave. I smelled this guy at the hotel! Sam peered out from under the truck. Looking up, she saw a beautiful white mustache and a neat gray suit.

Mustache! Relief spread through Sam's body.

She wriggled out and fell in step behind Mustache. *I wasn't really lost. I was just being clever. I was waiting for one of those spies to come by.*

Mustache stopped for a red light and Sam sat down behind him, careful to keep out of his view. When he crossed, she crossed. *A lot of dogs would have panicked.*

Threading through the crowds, Sam stayed close to Mustache. She was telling herself how brilliant she was when she saw limousines. *Ha! The hotel! Just like I planned.*

Edging closer to Mustache, Sam tried to look as if she was his dog.

"Good afternoon, sir," said the doorman politely. "Did you have a nice walk?"

"Very nice, thank you," said Mustache.

Sam stuck close to his heels so they'd think she was on a leash. The doorman looked at her oddly, but didn't say anything.

Keeping behind Mustache, Sam crossed the lobby. When they got to the elevators, she noticed a red sign exactly like the one that led to the stairs near Alexander's room. *Stairs!*

She dashed straight to the door and threw her weight against it. When it opened, Sam slipped into the stairwell. *No problem!*

She bounded up the stairs three at a time. Up and up she ran. Large numbers were painted on the brick wall on each floor. Sam looked at each one as she dashed past. *What do those stupid things say?*

Suddenly one caught her eye. A huge "10" was painted on the wall beside a door. *Hey! I know that one! A stick and a ball. That's our floor!*

Sam stood on her hind legs and pushed the bar on the door with her paws. The door opened and the crimson carpet of the tenth floor stretched before her. She dashed down the empty hallway, straight to suite 1014 and sniffed. *Open up, Jennie.* She scratched at the door.

Jennie opened the door with a puzzled look on her face. "How did you get out here, Sam?"

Beth peered around the door frame. "We thought you were sleeping in the bedroom."

You thought wrong.

"Come in here this minute!" Jennie was suddenly angry. "You said you wouldn't get in any trouble!" She folded her arms. "I should have known it was you who left the door open! I thought it was the maid!"

Sam sniffed as she marched past Jennie. *Worry, worry. Fuss, fuss. It's not as if you two were any help when I needed you.*

Jennie's mouth dropped open. "What did you do?"

But Sam just walked to the bedroom and

climbed up on the silk bedspread. *Call room service, Jennie. I'm starving.*

I want root beer. And crispy fried fish with butterscotch sauce and ketchup.

12. Who Are the Bad Guys?

Beth clutched her stomach. "Ugh."

Ketchup and butterscotch sauce dripped from Sam's chops as she crunched her fish.

I know why those spies are trading envelopes. Sam slurped up some sauce. *They're learning how to make nuclear bombs.*

"This is very scary." Jennie's face clouded.

Sam licked her chops calmly. *It's just like the movies — good guys against bad guys. Some evil genius wants to take over the world, so he sends his spies to find out how to make bombs.*

"Gosh." Jennie breathed deeply. "Take over the world!"

"I've seen lots of TV shows about that," said

Beth. "There's always someone who wants to make people into slaves." She narrowed her eyes and folded her arms firmly. "We should catch those spies and save the world."

Yeah. I'll get a big prize from the United Nations. Sam pictured herself in New York City getting a beautiful gold medal. Flags from every country fluttered against a bright blue sky. Cameras flashed.

"B-but we can't tell who the spies are." Jennie chewed her lip.

Beth was determined. "We'll watch to see who's stealing stuff. Then we'll know."

Sam's head whipped up. *The kid's brilliant. Well ... not as brilliant as me — but pretty smart.*

She looked sadly at her empty plate. *I wish I'd ordered more food.*

It wasn't easy to find out who was stealing secrets. Up and down the elevator, up and down the stairwell and back and forth through the lobby they went. But the three friends couldn't find out anything.

They went back up to the eleventh floor and watched the crowd milling around at the conference. But they couldn't get close enough to hear what people were saying.

Let's see what Alexander's doing.

On the tenth floor there was nothing in the hall but housekeeping carts.

I want to watch. Get behind that cart.

Jennie nudged Beth and they squeezed in between the wall and the cart.

"This is a very weird way to save the world," muttered Beth, peering around a pile of towels.

A woman in a big hat walked down the hall and went into a room.

Two maids came from the other direction, laughing and chatting. Then they got on the elevator and disappeared, leaving the hall empty again.

After a while the exit door opened a crack. Jennie and Beth waited. Sam held her breath.

Sneaky peered out. Behind him came Ear-Wire.

Aha! They use the stairs so nobody will see them.

Slowly the two spies opened the door and looked around the hallway. Then they stepped out, closed the exit door slowly and went noiselessly down the hall. At suite 1062, they stopped.

Hey! They're stopping at Alexander's!

Ear-Wire knocked but there was no answer. For a moment the two men listened. Then they nodded to each other. Ear-Wire produced a door card from his pocket and slid it into the lock.

Jennie, Beth and Sam didn't move.

Sneaky leaned in and called, "Dr. Jingawa! Are you here?"

No answer.

The two spies nodded to each other again. Then they stepped into the room.

With a tiny click, the door closed behind them.

And there was silence.

13. Into the Unknown

I'M GOING TO STOP THEM!

Sam's brain whirred. *They're the bad guys! They've broken into the room and they're spying on Alexander's father!*

Sam poked her head around the cart. *I'm going to stop them!*

Jennie paled. "Wait a m-minute. D-d-don't spies have guns?"

"Yeah," whispered Beth grimly. "They do."

I'll bite them. Did I ever tell you about my wonderful teeth?

Jennie clutched Sam tightly. "S-stay here. It's t-too dangerous."

"Look!" Beth hissed.

Out of Alexander's room came the two

spies. They closed the door with a quiet click. Without a word, they walked to the exit door and disappeared.

Sam jumped out from behind the cart. *Come on!*

She dashed to the exit door and threw her weight against it. *Hurry!*

Jennie and Beth followed Sam into the stairwell. They stood still for a moment, watching and listening.

Below them, they heard footsteps ringing on the concrete stairs.

Slowly, the three friends tiptoed down the stairs following the sound of the footsteps. Down, down, down. Like an old castle, the stairs were cold. Down, down, down.

Suddenly the echoing footsteps stopped.

Sam, Jennie and Beth froze.

A metal bar sounded and a door opened with a squeak.

Now this is getting interesting.

"They've opened a door down there," whispered Jennie.

"It must be the basement." Beth's voice was tiny.

Creeping a little farther down the stairs, Jennie and Beth clutched each other. The hallway was getting darker. Down ... down.

Around the next turn the stairs ended. The door at the bottom was closing very, very slowly.

Before Jennie could stop her, Sam darted through the door.

"Sam!" Jennie hissed. In horror she looked at Beth.

"Let's go," whispered Beth.

Together, Jennie and Beth slipped through the closing door.

Into the unknown.

14. Trapped!

SPIES ARE VERY TRICKY.

With a sighing sound, the door shut behind them. Jennie and Beth huddled together, waiting for their eyes to adjust to the dimness.

They were in a gloomy stone room with pipes running along the walls and ceiling. Sam was nowhere to be seen. Neither were the two spies.

Jennie reached for the door handle and pulled. Then she pushed. But the door wouldn't move. Her heart sank. "We can't get out," she whispered, grabbing Beth's arm.

Beth yanked at the door, but it wouldn't budge. "It locked behind us!"

Terror spread through Jennie's body. She

pulled on the door as hard as she could. Even her fingertips tingled with fear.

Beth pulled, too. "We're trapped!"

Spots swam before Jennie's eyes as she tugged at the door handle. It was no use.

Beth took a deep breath. "Okay. We're not going to panic," she announced firmly. "We'll find another way out." She peered into the gloom. "Where's Sam?"

"Sam!" whispered Jennie as loudly as she dared.

Stop wasting time. The spies went this way.

"I can hear her." Jennie slowly pointed to a brick doorway at the far end of the room. "She's in there."

Fearfully Jennie and Beth went toward the dark doorway. Gripping the door frame, they took a deep breath and stepped through it into another dim room. It looked like a dungeon in a haunted house.

Hearts pounding, they stood like statues while their eyes searched every corner.

"Where are the spies?" whispered Beth.

Something cold and wet burrowed into Jennie's hand. With a little shriek, she jumped.

Sam was disgusted. *What are you so nervous about?*

Jennie whirled on Sam. "Sam! You scared me!"

Sam looked up calmly. *Looks like we're stuck down here.*

"It sure does!" hissed Jennie. "And it's your fault."

Sam shrugged. *How was I supposed to know the door would lock?*

"Don't start one of your big conversations with Sam," whispered Beth, looking around fearfully. "We've got to find out where the spies went."

Sam jerked her head at an old wooden door.

"That way." Jennie pointed.

Very slowly they moved through the murky basement toward the closed door. Beth got to it first. She lifted the latch carefully and pulled. The door squealed. Jennie and Beth flinched.

Stop worrying. The spies have gone somewhere.

Jennie and Beth leaned through the doorway, their hearts in their mouths.

Come on. Quit stalling! I want to save the world.

The room was much bigger than the last two. Tables and chairs were stacked near the edges. There were four doors.

"W-w-which way should we go?" Jennie peered around the shadowy room nervously.

"Ask Sam. Maybe she can smell her way out."

But Sam was already disappearing through one of the doorways. *Speed it up, you two.*

"Dogs are good at finding their way," declared Beth.

"She'd better be. She got us into this," muttered Jennie. "I'm never ordering room service for her again."

Up ahead, Sam's ears twitched. *That's what you think. When I get back I'm having a cheese and chocolate sandwich with horseradish.*

Clinging together, Jennie and Beth followed Sam as she trotted through darkened doorway after doorway. Boxes, old furniture, huge chandeliers, boards and lampposts were stacked in every corner. The basement was enormous. Dark stone and cobwebs. Any kind of monster could be lurking here. Far from the world, far from the light, far from people — it was a basement where anything could happen.

"I think the spies wanted us to follow them," Beth said hollowly.

Jennie gulped. "You mean so they could trap us?"

Grimly, Beth nodded. "Yeah."

Then they heard it.

A chuckle came from somewhere. A nasty chuckle, filled with malice. Another chuckle joined in until the chuckles swelled into laughter.

"They've got us!" whispered Jennie.

Drat.

I forgot spies are so tricky.

15. They're after Us!

THOSE ARE TORTURE MACHINES!

Keep moving.

With pounding hearts and sweating hands, the girls followed Sam through the murky light. Laughter seemed to be coming from the stone walls.

Be quiet! All this laughing is getting on my nerves.

The basement went on forever in a maze of corridors and rooms.

We need a way out. I'm hungry.

Maybe I'll have steak. Sam's mouth watered at the thought of a juicy steak covered in ketchup and potato chips. *It's great to be rich.*

Jennie didn't answer. Her head was pounding and her eyes were blurry with fear. But the laughter seemed to be getting fainter.

"It doesn't sound like they're following us," whispered Beth.

"Do you think that's the spies laughing?"

Yup. Sam chortled to herself. *While they're telling dumb jokes we're getting away. But the joke's on them.*

Sam stepped through another doorway and the girls followed. They were in an enormous shadowy room filled with strange machines.

Sam jumped. *Yikes! It's the torture chamber!*

"T-t-torture?" squeaked Jennie.

Yeah. Don't you watch spy movies? Spies torture people to make them tell their secrets. On TV I saw spies stretching somebody's fingers and toes. Sam shivered. *I wonder if they do that to dogs.*

"Spies t-t-torture people?"

"Nobody's going to get tortured," said Beth bravely. "We're getting out of here."

"Sure." But Jennie didn't sound very sure.

They tiptoed around the machinery. Jennie shuddered. What if the spies caught them and stuffed them into these machines to twist their fingers and stretch their arms?

"Don't look at that stuff," ordered Beth firmly. "Keep going."

But Sam sniffed all the machines. *Hmm ... Oil ... Grease ... I can't tell what they're for. Not that it matters. What matters is getting back to the room and having a big fat steak.*

A loud thump came from somewhere.

They froze in their tracks.

Stay calm. I have wonderful teeth.

"Please, s-sniff your way out of here, Sam," begged Jennie.

Sam sniffed. All she could smell was moldy stones. *Forget the sniffing. Follow me.*

She led the girls past the torture machines into another cavernous room. At the far end, there was a strange door with an old-fashioned button beside it.

Hey! That's an elevator! Sam whirled around in happy circles. Prancing ahead, she lifted her head high. *I'm a genius! We're out of here! Time for my steak.*

Yahoo!

"S-S-Sam says that's an elevator," stammered Jennie.

A loud thud sounded behind them.

"Quick!" Beth grabbed Jennie and ran toward the doors. She whammed the button hard. "I hope you're right, Sam," she muttered.

Another thud.

Jennie shrieked.

Stop screaming! They'll catch us.

Wildly Jennie's eyes swept the room. There were five other doors. Which one would the spies come out of? Where were they?

Thud.

Beth leaned on the button. "Open up," she murmured with closed eyes. "Please, please be an elevator."

Thud. Thump.

Sam heaved her whole body against the doors. *Open up! Dangerous spies are after us. We can't stand around all day.*

Thump. Thump.

The three friends held their breath ...

Slowly, the doors creaked open.

16. Escape

WE'RE OUT OF HERE!

It was an old-fashioned wooden elevator.

I hope this thing works!

Frantically, Beth punched the "up" button. "Please, please go up."

Jennie leaned on the button that said "close." Very slowly the doors squealed together.

"Why won't this thing move!" Beth gritted her teeth and pressed the "up" button again and again.

Jennie squeezed her eyes shut and crossed her fingers.

It'll take a year to get upstairs at this rate.

Beth held the button down. At last the elevator shuddered.

Hurray! We're out of here!

The old elevator moved.

You didn't catch us, you crummy spies! Bye-bye, suckers!

"M-maybe we should w-wait until we're safe b-b-before we brag, Sam." Jennie watched the elevator doors with a worried look.

A little bragging never hurt anybody.

The elevator lurched upward.

Suddenly it ground to a stop.

We're here! Sam stepped from foot to foot in her happy little dance.

"M-maybe the spies ran up the stairs," whispered Jennie nervously. "M-m-maybe they're waiting for us."

"Yeah." Beth's eyes were glued to the doors.

The doors rattled open.

17. Sam Lands in Heaven

BOY, ARE THEY GROUCHY!

Jennie, Beth and Sam peeked around the door frame.

They were looking at a huge, gleaming steel kitchen. Cooks in white hats worked at endless stoves. Chefs ran to and fro with bowls. Some were stirring. Others were tasting. Nobody paid attention to the elevator tucked in an alcove.

Steamy, wonderful smells wafted into Sam's nose. *Wow! Do these people give snacks?*

"Don't let them see us, Sam," whispered Jennie. "We'll have to sneak out."

Too easy. Sam stepped off the elevator. Jennie and Beth followed.

No one in the busy kitchen looked up.

"Hide behind that big cupboard," hissed Beth.

They squeezed in behind the cupboard just as the elevator doors squeaked shut.

"Now, we'll go to that empty counter over there," whispered Beth. Jennie nodded.

Sam sniffed. A smell she loved made her shiver with delight. *Lemon pie.* She sniffed again. *Fried onions. I love lemon pie with fried onions.*

"Okay. Go to the counter," commanded Beth.

I need a snack.

"No snacks," said Jennie firmly. "We have to get back to our room."

"Yeah," added Beth. "We'll get in huge trouble if they catch us here. The kitchen is off limits."

Who cares about limits? I care about food. Sam sniffed again and her whole body quivered with happiness. *Cinnamon rolls. Mmmm.*

But the girls pulled Sam by the collar.

Okay. Okay. Sam followed her friends to a big stainless steel counter and crouched behind it. *Ah! Chicken soup.*

Jennie held Sam tightly.

People were running back and forth. A chef was having a temper tantrum about his sauce. He pulled off his chef's hat and threw it on the floor. Still nobody noticed Jennie, Beth and Sam.

"Next," Beth hissed, "is that table. Get ready."

Who cares about tables? Sam inhaled. *Strawberries. Mmmm ... There's caramel sauce here and sizzling steaks and warm buttered bread and crispy fish. I can't stand it!*

Jennie poked Sam in the ribs. "Stop it. We have to get out of the kitchen."

Don't poke me. I might bite.

"Never mind about biting," Jennie snapped. "Just do what we say."

Sam scowled at Jennie. *You're very bossy.*

Beth barked another order. "Get to the table."

Sam was getting grumpy. *Who made her the queen of the world?* A sudden smell hit her. *Roast chicken! I'm in heaven!*

Jennie pulled at Sam. Reluctantly, Sam

followed the girls to the table and crouched underneath it. They peered out at all the legs in white pants running back and forth.

"We have to go beside that cupboard next." Beth crept to the edge of the table. "Get ready."

Stop giving orders like an army sergeant. Sam turned away in disgust.

She breathed deeply and sighed. *Pumpkin pie. My absolute favorite. Warm pumpkin pie covered with ketchup ... Mmmm ... I'm starving to death.*

Without knowing it, Sam stood and moved toward the smell. *Mmm ... Mmmm ... Mmmmm ...* She closed her eyes and dreamed as she walked. *Pepperoni on pumpkin pie. Mmmmm.*

Bump! Sam ran into something hard. Annoyed, her eyes flew open. *So, where's the pie?*

Looking down at her from over a huge tray was a chef.

"A dog!" he screamed.

Heads whipped up from all over the kitchen. "A dog?"

Listen to them. You'd think I was a grizzly bear or something.

"Dog hair is disgusting. It gets in the food!" yelled another chef.

Watch what you say about my lovely fur.

A cook waved his hat at Sam. "Shoo! The health department will close the hotel!"

Shoo, yourself! You'd think I was a poisonous boa constrictor. I'm a beautiful dog and everyone loves me.

"Dogs have germs!" screamed a chef who was stirring soup. He waved his spoon, and a blob of soup landed at Sam's feet. She stooped to lap it up. *Ptooey. Mushroom.*

Sam raised her head and licked the side of a jam roll on the counter. *Not bad.*

Another chef lurched toward Sam waving a rolling pin.

Uh-oh. This guy looks violent.

"It's against the law to have a dog in a hotel kitchen!" he shrieked. "Put that dog out on the street!"

Sam stopped licking instantly. *Street? No way. It's a jungle out there. Forget the street.*

She wheeled around and started to run.

Shouting chefs came from all sides of the

kitchen and ran after Sam. Jennie and Beth peeked out from behind the island.

"Kids!" screamed one of the cooks.

"Throw them out, too!" roared a voice.

Sam ran for her life, with Jennie and Beth right behind her.

Somebody opened a swinging door, and Jennie, Beth and Sam shot out of the kitchen. Surprised people looked up from their tables.

With Sam in the lead, the three friends streaked through the restaurant.

"To the lobby," panted Beth. "Get to the elevators!"

Every head in the lobby looked up. The man in cowboy boots scowled as the three friends shot past.

"Why do they let dogs in hotels?" cried a woman wearing rhinestone sunglasses.

Jennie, Beth and Sam threw themselves into

an open elevator. Beth pressed the button. Instantly the doors closed and the elevator whooshed them upstairs.

Sam looked at her friends cheerfully.

Some fun, huh?

18. Sam Gets an Idea

I'LL CORNER THEM!

When they got back to the room, Sam insisted that Jennie order room service.

"You'd better hide, Sam," sighed Jennie. "Somebody might recognize us, and I don't want to get into trouble."

Sam sniffed. *Who cares about a little trouble?*

Before long there was a knock on the door. Sam had ordered a bacon burger with whipped cream. Jennie and Beth wanted plain bacon burgers.

Sam darted behind a sofa and sniffed. It smelled wonderful.

The waiter was apologetic. "I'm sorry, but we had some confusion in the kitchen. I don't think this is right."

Beth and Jennie lifted the food covers and peered at the plates. "Perfect," they both said.

The waiter's bushy black eyebrows shot up. "It can't be right! Nobody puts whipped cream on a bacon burger!"

We're rich. Nobody tells rich people what to eat.

Jennie smiled her toothiest smile. "That one's for me. I love it."

The waiter shook his head worriedly. "Maybe I should talk to your parents about the food you're ordering."

Nobody's talking to parents about anything.

"They're not here," said Jennie happily.

"Gone shopping," grinned Beth.

"Oh." The waiter hesitated.

Ask this guy if he's leaving any time soon.

"Well, okay then." Still shaking his head, the waiter finally left.

Sam came out from behind the sofa, chuckling. *That guy doesn't know anything about good food.*

When Sam finished her burger, she burped

loudly. *Now, back to the mystery of the evil spies.* She licked her chops. *I'll catch them tonight.*

Jennie clutched at her head. "Sam's still determined to catch the spies, Beth!"

Beth grinned at Sam. "Me, too."

Sam looked lovingly at Beth. *Beth's great. But tell her I'm getting the United Nations medal. She'd better not try to grab it just because I'm a dog.*

Jennie groaned.

Waiting behind the housekeeping cart in the hall was boring. *We've been here for ten minutes. I need some excitement.* Sam scratched herself with her hind leg.

"Sit still, Sam," ordered Beth.

Sam glared. *Still acting like the queen of the world, I see.*

At that moment the exit door opened and Ear-Wire and Sneaky appeared.

They are sneaking away from the conference again.

The two spies looked up and down the hall before they headed for Alexander's door. Sneaky pulled out his stolen door card, unlocked the door, and they let themselves in again.

Look at those guys! They steal stuff all the time!

Just then the elevator doors opened and a different waiter pushed out a room service table.

When he got near the housekeeping cart, he stopped and flipped open a note pad. "Suite 1062. Right here." He looked at his pad and checked the table. "Bucket of ice." He tipped over an empty bucket.

Sam squinted at the long tablecloth. *That is exactly what I need.*

The waiter sighed and took the empty bucket down the hall into an alcove. Jennie, Beth and Sam heard ice cubes clinking.

Perfect!

Before Jennie could stop her, Sam shot out from their hiding place and dove under the tablecloth. *See you later, Jennie. I've got spies to catch.*

Helplessly, Jennie and Beth watched the waiter wheel the cart to suite 1062. The bottom of the tablecloth wiggled suspiciously.

Ear-Wire opened the door. "I'll take it from here," he said.

"He's pretending to be Dr. Jingawa!" whispered Beth.

Jennie watched the waiter go back to the elevator. Then she heard Sam's thoughts, and her heart sank.

I'll corner these spies with my wonderful teeth.

Jennie grabbed Beth. "Sam says she's going to corner the spies!"

Beth gasped. "I don't think that's a good idea!"

"It's a terrible idea! Sam's going to get us all killed!"

The bottom of the tablecloth wiggled again, and the girls caught a glimpse of Sam's feet. Ear-Wire pushed the table into the room, and the door closed with a click.

"What do we do now?" whispered Jennie. "Sam's trapped in there!"

Minutes crawled by. It seemed as if Sam had been in that room forever.

"M-m-maybe they threw S-Sam out the window," stammered Jennie.

Beth paled. "That's what spies do in movies!"

Jennie chewed her lip unhappily. "Sam's in real trouble, Beth."

Beth took a deep breath. "But she's got us," she said fiercely. "We'll get her out."

"How?"

Beth eased herself out from behind the cart and listened at the room. She motioned for Jennie to join her.

When Jennie put her ear to the door, she heard Sam's thoughts clearly. *These guys are boring, Jennie. All they do is look out the window.*

"Sam says it's boring."

They're not doing any spy stuff. Get me out of here.

"She wants to get out."

"Yeah." Beth clenched her small fists. "But how?"

Throw a blanket over these guys. That'll give us time to escape! Then we'll call the police.

Jennie sighed. "She wants us to throw a blanket over them."

"It might work."

Jennie's eyebrows shot up. "Are you crazy?"

But Beth was serious. "This is how we'll do it. First, we knock on the door and say we've got a message."

"W-what kind of message could k-kids have?"

Beth thought hard. "We'll say we've got something to tell Alexander."

Furrowing her brow, Beth chewed harder on her fingernail. Then she snapped her fingers. "We'll ask to write it down! Then we'll throw blankets over their heads and Sam can do the rest! She's always telling you about her wonderful teeth."

"Y-you want to throw blankets over a couple of spies!"

"Yup." Beth was firm. "It's the only way."

Jennie felt faint. "They'll tie us up!"

Beth clenched her fists again. "We can't let them have Sam."

Jennie thought for a moment. The idea of losing Sam was too terrible to think about. "I-I g-guess we have no choice."

Hello-o! Are you listening? Hurry up! I'm bored in here if anybody cares. Hello-o.

Beth was already taking two blankets off the housekeeping cart. "Do you have your room card ready?" she whispered.

Jennie nodded as she took one of the blankets.

"Good. We'll need to get out fast, so prop the door open. Then we'll run to our room and hide."

Beth knocked. After a minute the door opened and Ear-Wire looked down at them. "What do you kids want?"

"Is Alexander here?" said Beth in a loud voice.

Ear-Wire shook his head and started to close the door.

"Could we please leave him a note?" Beth

asked politely, but loudly.

Ear-Wire looked annoyed. Suddenly, he shrugged. "Why not? Write it on the message pad by the phone."

Ear-Wire let them in and nodded to the phone table on the other side of the room. Then he went back to the window, where Sneaky was watching something through binoculars. They had their backs to the girls.

From under the cloth on the room service table, Jennie could see the tip of Sam's paw sticking out.

About time you got here! Do you have any idea how boring it is to be stuck under a cart?

While Beth pretended to write on the message pad, Jennie propped the room door open, ready for a quick escape.

"It'll take me a minute to write it all down!" Beth yelled.

"Take your time, kid," said Sneaky, without turning around.

"Sam!" Jennie leaned over and whispered to the cart. "You were really crazy to come in here."

Never mind that! Throw the blankets over these boring guys! Sam's head poked out. *Maybe I should bite them.*

Frantically Jennie grabbed Sam. "Forget the blankets. Let's go!" she hissed, pointing to the open door.

Sam slid out from under the cart. *All right. All right.*

"Hurry!" Jennie shoved Sam from behind.

No need to get pushy.

Beth glanced at the spies' backs. "Run!" she mouthed.

Okay. I'll corner those guys later.

Sam raced for the door, with Jennie and Beth close behind.

"Oof!" Sam ran through the open door — right into someone's legs.

"What's this!" cried a voice.

Shouts echoed through the hallway.

"A dog!"

"What's it doing in our room?"

"Who are these kids?"

Sam had run straight into the Jingawa family.

19. We're out of Here!

Dr. Jingawa clutched his briefcase. "What's the meaning of this!"

I'll tell you the meaning. It's time to go!

Sam crashed through Dr. Jingawa's legs and bolted for the stairs. *Follow me!*

Dr. Jingawa was so surprised he stopped yelling.

Jennie and Beth dashed after Sam. As they darted down the hall, they heard someone call, "Stop those kids!"

Shouts echoed behind them as Jennie and Beth raced after Sam. Heaving herself against the door, Sam wedged through and started down the stairs.

Down, down, down they went. Numbers flashed by as they turned at each floor. Voices echoed from above.

"Darn kids!"

"Stop!"

But the three friends didn't stop. Around and around they went! Down, down, down. When Sam got to the street door, she leaped up and crashed against the bar with her paws.

It flew open! In a flash, she was out. Crowds milled around her. Cars honked. People rushed past. But Sam didn't notice. Her eyes were fixed on the door as she waited for her friends.

Then they were there. Beth and Jennie tumbled out the door into the sunlight, and looked around in surprise.

"Woof!" *Over here!* Sam was waiting at the edge of the sidewalk. *Hurry! We'll get lost in the crowd.*

Threading their way through the people, Jennie and Beth rushed over to Sam.

Here's the plan. Back to the lobby, up the elevator and straight to our own room.

"Come on, Beth," said Jennie. "We'll go through the lobby."

Sam stayed close to the girls when they got to the hotel's front doors. *Pretend I'm on a leash.*

"Hello, young ladies," said a doorman in a friendly way. "Have you been out sightseeing?"

Jennie and Beth smiled and nodded.

"Hope you had a good time," the other doorman said. Then he looked at Sam. "Wait a minute. Is that your dog?"

Jennie and Beth nodded again.

The doorman scratched his head. "I could have sworn I saw this dog with Dr. Damodar a few hours ago."

Uh-oh. Sam lowered her head and tried to droop like a spaniel.

"Must have been a different sheepdog," Beth piped up as she rushed Sam through the door. "Heh, heh. I heard there was a dog here that looked like ours." She smiled brilliantly at the doorman. "See you later, sir."

Sam drooped more. But the doorman scratched his head again. "That dog looks exactly like Dr. Damodar's dog."

Who cares what I look like, Nosy.

Luckily a limousine pulled up just then and the doorman was gone.

That guy should mind his own business.

"What's this about some doctor?" Jennie asked suspiciously as they crossed the lobby.

The doorman needs glasses.

But Jennie narrowed her eyes at Sam. "What happened when you disappeared?"

Never mind that. Let's get to the room. Spy catching makes me hungry.

"We're not going to do any more spy catching, Sam," said Jennie firmly as she pushed the elevator button. "You made a mess of it."

Sam gasped. *I made a mess of it? It wasn't me who was too chicken to throw a blanket!*

They stepped onto the elevator. Whoosh. They were on the tenth floor.

When the door opened, Beth leaned out and looked cautiously up and down the hall. "There's nobody around." Nervously they tiptoed down the empty hallway to suite 1014.

As soon as they were inside, they all heaved a sigh of relief. Jennie flopped on the sofa and Beth sagged into a chair.

"I don't want another close call like that. Ever!" cried Jennie.

Don't be a wimp. Good detectives always have close calls.

Jennie glared at her. "We didn't catch any spies, Sam. We almost got caught ourselves."

Sam yawned. *Relax. I'll nab them after I've had a snack. I'm going to be the dog who saved the world. The most famous dog on the planet. Everyone will know about Sam — the dog who captured the dangerous nuclear spies.*

Sam sighed as she pictured her medal from the United Nations. People from every country in the world clapped and cheered. *Wonderful!*

Her daydream faded when the door opened.

20. The Truth about Dr. Jingawa

"Hi, kids!" called Jennie's mother. "Have you been bored?"

Jennie's mother and father bustled into the room, loaded with bags.

"The shopping was wonderful!" said Mrs. Levinsky, as she heaped her parcels on a chair.

Jennie's father fell on a sofa. "My feet will never be the same."

Just then Noel and Jason burst in. "The music stores are awesome!" Noel whipped CDs out of a bag. "We're going to listen to them all!"

They disappeared into their room with their earphones. The door shut firmly.

How about a little room service? Sam looked at Jennie happily. *Maybe some chocolate-covered lobster?*

Jennie was about to answer when there was a loud knock on the door.

Mrs. Levinsky opened the door. "Yes?" she said pleasantly.

Ear-Wire, Sneaky, Dr. Jingawa, Mrs. Jingawa and Alexander poured into the room.

Jennie's heart sank like a stone.

Beth gasped.

Uh-oh. Sam ran for the bedroom and crawled under the bed.

Sam tried to cover her ears, but she could still hear the voices.

"... intruders in our room."

"... inexcusable behavior!"

"... said they wanted to write a note."

Nuclear spies are such liars. They'll get us in a pile of trouble.

More voices wafted into the bedroom.

"... dog was in the kitchen!"

"… against the health laws."

"… dogs need discipline."

Sam pricked up her ears. *No way. I won't stand for discipline.*

The voices stopped.

We're going to save the world and you can't stop us. Sam crawled out from under the bed and peeked into the living room. Jennie's parents stood in furious silence. Jennie and Beth perched nervously on the edge of a sofa. To one side stood Ear-Wire, Sneaky and the Jingawas, their arms folded.

Sam sighed. *This is going to be boring. I can feel a big lecture coming.*

Sam sat down beside Jennie's knee. *You should have thrown that blanket. They'd be in jail right now and we'd be heroes.*

Mrs. Levinsky's angry voice broke into Sam's thoughts. "Speak up, Jennie. Just what have you girls been doing!"

"We want answers." Mr. Levinsky's jaw twitched angrily.

Neither Jennie nor Beth could speak. Their

faces flushed hot. For a long moment everyone glared at them.

This is a good time to be a dog.

At last Ear-Wire sat down. "There's no point in being angry," he said. "I need to understand the situation."

He leaned toward Jennie and Beth in a friendly way. "Look, kids, just tell us what's going on. We won't be mad if you tell us the truth." He looked at Jennie's parents. "Isn't that right, Mr. and Mrs. Levinsky?"

Never trust a spy, Jennie.

"Well ... all right. But we want the truth," said Jennie's father firmly.

"And we'll try not to be angry," added her mother.

"Um ..." Jennie squirmed miserably. "It's like this ... uh ... W-we found spies in the h-hotel," she answered at last.

"Nuclear spies," blurted Beth, trying to be helpful.

Jennie started to sweat.

There was another long silence. All the

adults looked at one another in disbelief.

Ear-Wire and Sneaky leaned forward, interested. "Who are the spies?"

"Um." Jennie flushed bright red. "You are." She gulped.

"Me! I work for hotel security!"

What about Sneaky here?

"W-what about h-him?" Jennie nodded nervously at Sneaky.

"We're both hotel security," answered Sneaky. "That's why we wear this two-way radio." He indicated his ear wire. "So we can talk to each other when we see something suspicious."

Okay ... So, what about the doctor?

Jennie nudged Beth. "Ask about Dr. Jingawa, Beth. I feel stupid doing all the talking," she whispered.

Beth took a deep breath. "Excuse me," she said politely, "but what about Dr. Jingawa? People have been stealing stuff from his room and delivering secret envelopes."

Tell them about the way he hangs on to his briefcase.

"And he w-won't let anybody touch his briefcase," put in Jennie. "It l-looked like spies to us," she finished lamely.

It is spies. Nuclear spies.

Everyone gaped at the girls. Alexander smirked nastily.

"Just what did you think the spies were doing?" asked Jennie's father at last.

"Stealing nuclear secrets," said Beth bravely. "All those people at the conference are talking about nuclear stuff. You know — bombs."

Tell them we were trying to save the world. They'll see how important our work is.

"W-w-we wanted to save the world," stammered Jennie.

"Save the world!" jeered a voice. Noel and Jason stood at their bedroom door with their earphones hanging around their necks. "You two must be the stupidest kids in the world!" Laughing uproariously, they went back into their room.

Sam sniffed. *Never listen to a pimply faced teenage oaf.*

"We need to explain a few things," said Sneaky. "First, they're not talking about nuclear bombs. It's a conference on nuclear medicine. X-ray technology, CAT scans — things like that."

Jennie felt her face get hotter and hotter.

"Dr. Jingawa is the main speaker at the conference. He's world famous and he's here to share his discoveries with scientists from sixty-seven countries."

Hmph. A likely story. So why does he clutch his briefcase like a spy?

"W-why does he hold on to his briefcase like there's a secret in it?" asked Jennie timidly.

"My lecture notes," declared Dr. Jingawa. "I keep them with me at all times. If I lost them, the conference would be ruined."

"We keep a copy of everything in our suitcase," added Mrs. Jingawa. "But he still gets nervous."

"What about the secret envelope the man with the mustache brought to your door?" asked Beth nervously.

"It's a scientific conference. We're here to share information and ideas," answered Dr. Jingawa. "Many of the scientists brought their own research. Alexander here does the photocopying for us."

Alexander stared at Jennie and Beth as if they were completely crazy.

Forget the kid. I never liked him anyway.

Jennie and Beth looked at each other.

Then Beth thought of something. "Excuse me, Dr. Jingawa, but would you mind answering one more question?"

Dr. Jingawa murmured, "Of course not."

Beth clasped her hands nervously. "What about these two men going into your room when you're not there?" She pointed to Sneaky and Ear-Wire. "It sort of looked like they were stealing something."

Sneaky and Ear-Wire burst out laughing. "We're not stealing anything!" they cried. "We're hotel security! Our job is to stop people from stealing!"

As if we believe that.

But Jennie did believe it. "You mean, you were trying to protect Dr. Jingawa?"

"Exactly. There are all kinds of industrial spies who would love to sneak into this conference and steal Dr. Jingawa's discovery. They could sell it for a lot of money."

Sam's head whipped up. *Spies! What did I tell you?*

"In fact," continued Ear-Wire, "when you saw us, we were watching some very suspicious activity in the building across the street."

"It's our job to make sure Dr. Jingawa is not spied upon in any way. His invention will be a great help to medicine when it's perfected," added Sneaky.

All eyes looked at Jennie and Beth.

They just squirmed.

At last everyone got up and said good-bye to Mr. and Mrs. Levinsky. The adults all shook hands and Jennie's parents apologized for the trouble.

As the Jingawas left the room, there were chuckles about children's imaginations. When Sneaky laughed, Sam's ears pricked up. She'd heard that laugh before — in the basement.

In misery, Jennie and Beth slumped on the sofa. They both glared at Sam.

"You sure got us in trouble this time, Sam," whispered Jennie through gritted teeth.

But Sam was humming happily to herself. *You weren't paying attention to Ear-Wire.*

There ARE spies around here.

I knew it.